SUPER S

adventures

THE FUN BEGINS

KRITHI
MUNAGALA

PUBLISHING & COPYRIGHTS

www.kreativekrithi.com

ISBN **978-0-692-12315-7**

For information, please email : kreativekrithi@gmail.com

ACKNOWLEDGEMENT

I would like to express my sincere gratitude to everyone who has helped me in my journey to create my first book, especially my pet, Sushi, for inspiring me to write this story.

Thanks to Vinay Abhishek, Independent Writer, for his encouragement and guidance in helping me get started on this journey.

I would like to thank Priyanka Misra, Publishing Consultant for her editing and guidance and Melanie Lopata, Children's Author and Freelance Editor, for her stylistic editing giving my book a professional outlook.

I wish to also express my thanks to Ganga and Bala Gopal, Independent Artists and Designers, for helping me bring out the characters to life through their spirited illustration of the characters and scenes.

Finally, I would like to thank my parents, teachers, friends and family for all their love, support and encouragement, without whom this book wouldn't have been possible.

ABOUT THE AUTHOR

Krithi Munagala is a 9-year-old budding writer from Sacramento, California. She is a creative ball of energy, who loves to write and create stories and poems by observing her surroundings. She is also learning piano and hopes to one day create songs out of her poems. Krithi is also very passionate about animals. Her dream is to become a writer, an Animal Rights lawyer and start a Pet Rescue home. The central theme of her poems and stories are around love, hope, happiness, strength and self-confidence. She wishes to spread these gems of life through her work.

CONTENTS

CREDITS

Author: Krithi Munagala

Illustrations & Designer: Ganga and Krithi Munagala

Cover Designer: Ganga and Bala Gopal

Edited by: Vinay Abhishek, Priyanka Misra, Melanie Lopata, Sirisha Munagala

Other Contributors: Anshu Shrivastava

PREFACE

Hi, my name is Krithi and this is my dog Sushi and my neighbour's dog Trixie.

I am nine years old, Sushi is one, and Trixie is about seven years old. I love writing and I am crazy about dogs. And so, I wanted to write a story about Sushi and Trixie.

When I first met Sushi, I felt something was very special about him. He is very loving, gives hugs and licks to everyone and brings a lot of happiness to everyone around him. He becomes a popular dog wherever he goes. So, I thought I should create a story about him. This is my first book and I wish to write many more.
I hope you enjoy this one!

Sushi and I

I live in a beautiful neighbourhood that is full of greenery and has plenty of walking trails. We have lots of friends around our house and we always do fun activities together. I love bicycling around and exploring the neighbourhood.

Tomorrow is Independence Day and we are going on a picnic with our neighbours. I know it is going to be so much fun. Sushi and I oversee snacks. Oops, how rude of me to not introduce you to the cutest little thing, my dog, Sushi. He is a white Maltese and is one year old. He is also very good friends with Trixie, our neighbour's dog. Trixie is seven years old and is a Maltese Poodle.

Sushi and I are planning to bring some juice and fruit for the picnic. We are also planning to bring some cupcakes. We aren't sure about it though, as Mom is super strict about sugar. Sigh! But we will try and convince her. I can't wait for tomorrow.

Well, it's getting late. I better wash up, finish dinner and get to bed. See you tomorrow!

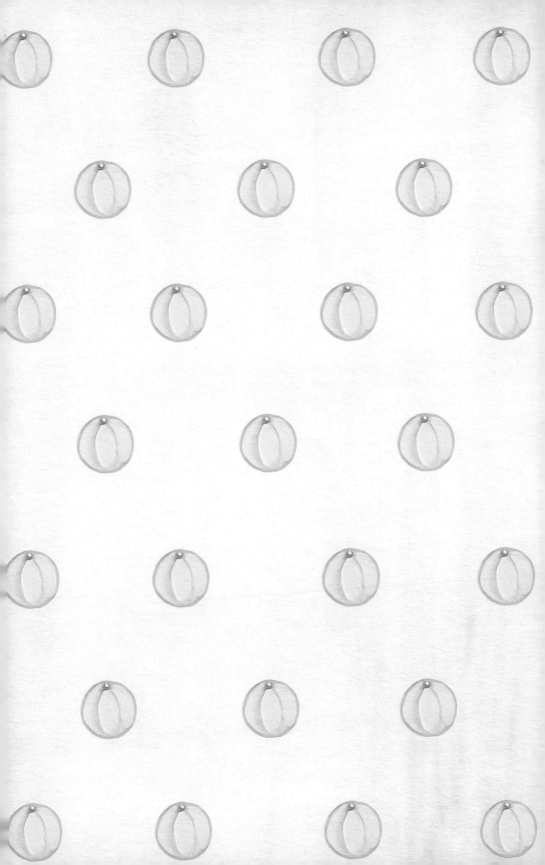

Picnic with Our Neighbours

I am super excited for today's picnic!! I hardly ate anything last night because I was in a rush to get to bed so I could wake up early. I am super hungry now. Need to have breakfast quickly.

Today is Independence Day. It's a beautiful day outside, just perfect for a picnic. Mom is busy preparing lunch and Dad is busy helping her pack. I had already prepared my snacks in a snack bag last night and I also packed some fun treats for Sushi and Trixie. And guess what? Mom said yes for the cupcakes. Yay! The snack department is all set.

Sushi and I quickly get ready and run out
to see if our neighbour friends are ready.
I see them all waiting outside, just
locking up. They are a family of five.
Trixie, their Maltese poodle,
is excited, too.

Mom and dad came out as well
and we all said our hellos, the
dogs greeted with their barks,
and we were on our way to the
picnic spot. The picnic
spot is near a beautiful
trail right behind our
house.

It took us less than ten minutes to get to the picnic spot.
We set up the blankets, food and drinks. Everything
smelled so great and yummy. The weather was
great with a nice cool breeze. I took a piece of
pie and ran to sit by the big tree right next to
our picnic spot and get my feet wet in the
cool water trickling down the stream.

Just as I was about to take a bite of the pie, I saw Trixie and Sushi running far away from the picnic spot. I panicked and quickly ran right behind them. I ran fast and just when I was about to get a hold of them, I tripped over something and fell with a loud BOOM! I hit a soft floor. The next thing I knew, Sushi and Trixie were on top of me.

03

The Pleasant Surprise

After the sudden fall, I woke up to a big surprise. I was in a strange room, big and colourful. I looked around and saw a lot of computers and electronic gadgets. There was a big screen on the wall with the world map and lots of red blinking dots on it.

But strangely, the room also had a fun looking bounce house, a rainbow coloured lazy chair, and a very inviting bed next to it. It looked like a spy's den. Suddenly, a tiny robot-like thing came walking up to me and started talking.

"Hello, I am Pop, your robot-friend." Everyone gasped.

"Who? What? Where?" My mind was still buffering from the fall. Finally, Sushi ran forward and started barking at the robot. It seemed as if he was communicating something. The robot responded as if it understood everything Sushi was saying. I was too shocked to say anything.

The robot said, "I know lil' puppy, you all want to know where you are and what all of this is about. It is going to surprise and shock you, but you all are here because you are special. You are the Super Heroes, chosen to help save this world from villains. This is your secret base and I am your assistant."

I kept thinking that all of this was a joke, perhaps a dream. I slowly stood up and looked around. It surely didn't look like a dream.

"You are pulling our leg, right?" I asked, finding my voice.

"No, I am not," the robot replied.

"But where did this all come from? Why us? We are just kids. How can we save the world?"

"I know, this is a lot for you all. But Dr. Freckles created this many years ago. He was a very smart scientist, but he suddenly just disappeared one night. We have tried a lot to find him, but we have not been successful.

He always wanted his invention to help stop all the bad things from happening around the world. This special antenna here can scan through all the computer systems in the country and detect any problem that is about to happen. And if there is no help around, it will send an alarm immediately so that the Super Heroes team can jump in and quickly help fight the problem."

"But why us?" I challenged.

"Dr. Freckles designed this in such a way that only those who are capable and truly deserving will find this place," Pop answered.

"It's great that we can help solve the problems, but how can we fight? We don't have any special powers."

"Well, that's not true," Pop said with a smile. "Here are some interesting parts of this fun ride. Here are your special costumes, and as soon as you wear these costumes you will get some super powers. So, Sushi and Trixie will be able to talk. They can talk to humans as well as to any animal."

Trixie ran towards a rainbow-colored costume, and Sushi immediately grabbed a blue-coloured one (he loves blue just like I do). I helped both get into their costumes. They looked cute.

"This is so cool!" Sushi exclaimed.

Trixie agreed. "Wow, I love this. I feel so strong."

I shook my head with an unbelievable look. "No way. I can understand
Sushi and Trixie." I ran to get my costume, just hoping it's not pink.
Guess what? It's blue and black, my favourite, and it fits me perfectly.

Pop continued to explain. "Sushi will have laser sharp eyes and can look up to 3,000 miles and Trixie can hear even a pin drop across the country. Krithi, you can run to another country in less than ten seconds. And most importantly, all of you can fly. Here's the fun surprise...you will have your own special vehicle called 'Squishy'. Squishy can turn into any vehicle you want - a car, a bike, a submarine, or a jet - and it has features to camouflage itself. It can also bake and deliver special super power cupcakes whenever you are hungry on your journey."

"Cupcakes! Hooray!" I shouted.

"Hey, what about us? We need treats too," Sushi said.

"I am hungry all the time," Trixie added.

Pop laughed. "Of course, you can also have the cupcakes."

Just as Pop was explaining all the fun features of Squishy, a loud siren went off.

"Alright Super Heroes, your first assignment is here. Time to go!"

"But wait - right now? Our family is outside at a picnic and they will probably be worried about us," I said, feeling shocked.

"Don't worry. I can make it appear to them that you and the dogs are playing nearby. I will help delay that until you get back," Pop assured us.

"How can you do that?"

Pop laughed at that. "I have a software to make it do that. It's called Virtual Reality."

"Wow!" Sushi said. "But wait...what if we are not able to save? What if we are in danger?"

"Don't worry; like I said, you are chosen for this job. You have all the powers. Any time you sense trouble, just use this 'Home' button on Squishy or on your costume and you will be back here. Trust me, it is always hard the first time. Next time you will be a pro."

Then Pop added, "Oh, almost forgot, you all have Super special names: Super Sushi, Terrific Trixie and Kool Krithi!"

"Wow," I said. "These are some awesome, pawsome names." (Everyone giggles.)

"One final and important point. The leader of your pack is Super Sushi."

"What? But I am the youngest and tiniest of all. How can I be the leader?" Sushi argued.

"Sushi, it doesn't matter how old, big, or small you are. You just need to believe in yourself," Pop replied.

"Wow, all this is so exciting, but scary, too," I said.

The alarm rang and there was a voice, "Cat Catastrophe, east side, 200 miles, Sugar City. Danger approaching in 30 minutes. Can damage human race and animal kingdom."

A Tough Battle

It was time to go on our first adventure. Pop could clearly see we were all nervous.

"Don't worry guys," Pop assured us. "Since this is your first assignment, I will be watching you and can control your actions with this special button on your costumes. If you are in trouble, I will immediately teleport you home."

Pop giving us courage was very comforting to us.

"Thank you, Pop," Sushi told him. "You are very encouraging. Krithi, Trixie, c'mon - we must be brave and strong. How many get such an opportunity? We all need to do our bit to protect the world in our own way."

"Uhhh...you are right, Sushi," I said, still lost because I can't get over Sushi talking. It is like a dream to me.

"You are right, buddy, let's do this," Terrific Trixie agreed.

"Excellent. Good luck, guys!" Pop waved us off.

"Alright, everyone into the Squishy NOW!" Super Sushi exclaimed.

As soon as we jumped into Squishy, we zoomed off in a second like a spaceship. We arrived a few miles away from Sugar City in less than a minute.

Squishy spoke through speakers. "Sugar City, 100,000 residents, main occupation Sugarcane farming and cattle rearing. Cat Catastrophe attacking to overtake the farms, sugar factories and cattle. Cat Catastrophe is driving unbreakable vehicles that can shoot out poisonous gas and can destroy human and animals in seconds."

"Oh! That sounds dangerous," I said.

We could clearly see a lot of evil-looking people dressed up as cats to cover their identity. They were approaching Sugar City in full speed. We had to act fast.

Super Sushi, who could clearly see up to 3000 miles, said "Guys, Cat Catastrophe is approaching from all directions. We need to be smart and destroy them in their vehicle. Okay, so here's the plan."
(Sushi discusses the plan with Trixie and I.)

"Sounds excellent! Let's move it," Terrific Trixie and I said.

"Guys," I said. "Remember, we can all camouflage. How about we split up, camouflage and attack? Remember the saying 'Divide and conquer'?"

"Great idea, Krithi," Super Sushi agreed. "I think we will catch them by surprise. Alright guys, no time to waste; let us use our flying power and get moving."

We all split up, used our flying buttons, and off we zoomed. Sushi quickly marked out the attack area a little away from the Cat Catastrophe's path and as soon as the car came into the zone, within seconds, he used his super powers to turn the poisonous gas emitter into the vehicle and activated the release button.

BOOM! SMACK! In no time the vehicle and everyone inside was destroyed. Success!!!

Sushi quickly moved over to the others to follow the same attack.

Trixie and I followed the same and soon all the villains were destroyed before they could even enter Sugar City.

We could hear the police arriving and we realized we needed to get back soon.

Pop's voice came over via the remote. "Guys, time to leave the scene. The police are arriving. Get back to Squishy. I'll get you home."

We quickly flew back to Squishy and gave each other a high five. Wow, what an experience! We couldn't believe that we fought the bad guys successfully.

In less than a minute we were all back to the base.

A Great Idea

As we landed back to the base, it felt so good.

"Oh my gosh!" Pop exclaimed. "That was amazing, guys. See, I told you, you didn't need my help."

"Thank you, Pop. I think you prepared us well," Super Sushi answered.

I agreed. "It was unbelievable. But it was also a very hard fight." Then I said, after a thought, "Pop, are our parents okay? I hope they are not worried."

"Don't worry, they did call out for you a couple of times and I responded on your behalf saying you are playing with Trixie and Sushi."

"Great!"

Terrific Trixie chimed in. "Yes, it was quite a fight. But I have a question. I am sure there are a lot of people and animals who need help all over the world, right? How can we be there around the world at the same time? We three are not enough to fight everything that is going on at the same time in different places around the world."

"That is so true. We would have to be flying across the globe all the time. And even then, I am not sure if that's enough," I told Pop.

"You all are right," Super Sushi said. "We can't do all this fighting alone, right? I think I have an idea. What if we go all around the world once, and just like how we formed a group, talk to our animal friends; and Krithi can talk to her human friends and create groups like ours in different parts of the world. Then each of us can help protect the part of the world we live in."

"That is an excellent idea, Sushi. You are now talking like a true leader. I am so glad I found you. Dr. Freckles would have been so proud of your team today."

Sushi's eyes were glowing with pride.

Terrific Trixie and I agreed. "What a great idea, Sushi!"

"But I think it will be quite a bit of hard work to go all over the world. We need to plan this out really well," Super Sushi told us.

"Don't worry," Pop assured us. "I can help you with planning and the super-fast travel part."

"We can decide on the places to go to which can cover every part of the world," I suggested.

Pop nodded. "I can give you teleporting powers and special head-phones, so I can communicate with you wherever you guys are in the world. Your costume allows communication only until a certain distance. I can also give you remotes with matching maps based on your team, so you can try finding matching teams around the world."

"That sounds perfect!" Super Sushi exclaimed.

"Excellent. So, when do we go? I am so excited for this mission," Terrific Trixie said, jumping up and down.

"Alright, let us plan this tomorrow. It is your first day today; I think you all need some rest. Tomorrow we can discuss the plan and get started. I think we can try to cover the world in about one week. I just hope we don't get too many assignments in between," Pop told us.

I grinned. "Awesome! Sounds great! It's my summer break and this will be an excellent way to spend my holidays. But for now, I think we better get back to our picnic."

Super Sushi and Terrific Trixie laughed. "Yes, and we better take off our costumes."

All of us quickly change.

"Alright guys, see you tomorrow," Pop waved to us.

"Bye Pop, see you tomorrow," I said as I waved back.

Sushi & Trixie barked. "Woof, woof," (wishing Pop goodbye in their dog language I guess.)

We all get back to our picnic spot.

Mom and Dad looked concerned. "What did you guys do for so long?"

"Ahh...well...we were having some Cat Catastrophe fun," I said with a giggle, winking at Sushi and Trixie.

CHAPTER

06

Around the World

I woke the next morning and for a moment, I felt like everything that happened yesterday was part of a dream. But then I noticed Sushi. He was waiting by the bedside, moving his head and body as if he was telling me that he is ready to leave.

Oh my gosh! That is no dream. We must get to our Secret Base. Today we start our journey around the world to build the Super World Team.

I quickly got ready and rushed to the kitchen, gobbled some milk and cereal, and ran out to the Secret Base. I told Mom that I was working on a fun project with Sushi and Trixie, borrowed her spare phone, and wore my GPS watch for safety. Sushi and Trixie always had their GPS collars, so they were covered on the safety part as well. Safety, all check!

As soon as we reached the Secret Base, Trixie was already there. Thank goodness - we almost forgot about her.

Pop greeted us. "Welcome guys. Are you all set? Let us get started fast so you can get back home before your parents get worried. Here is the plan for the next five days. All these stops will make sure you cover the entire world. Today will be the longest since you will be travelling the farthest. Also, here is your mapping remote.

I put all your information in this, so whenever you scan someone with this remote, you will see a green light if it matches. Otherwise, you see a red light. This can help you build your teams quickly around the world. Here is a bag full of Squishy pop-ups and costumes for your teams. Good Luck!"

We all quickly change into our Super Hero suits and jump into Squishy, which zoomed off in a second.

Our first stop was China. As we zoomed past all the cities, we kept the remote activated. We quickly found our team; a beagle named Chubby, a white fluffy cat named Dumpling, and a 10-year-old boy named David. Of course, they were all as shocked as we were. Sushi and Trixie communicated everything in animal language and I explained to David. They were proud to be the Super Heroes of China. We wished the China team luck and set out to our next country, India.

The green light was beeping a lot in India and we were getting very confused. But we finally managed to put together a team of a German Shepherd named Rustom, a Shitzhu named Robin, and an 11-year-old girl named Ariana. Team India Super Heroes was all set.

Our next stop was Japan, where we found two dogs - Leo, a Spitz, and Mochi, a Chow Chow - and our human member, Sara, a 10-year-old. Team Japan Super Heroes was ready to roll.

Our final stop of the day was the United Kingdom (U.K.), where the team was a pink pig named Happy, a Labrador named Butterscotch, and a 9-year-old boy named Peter. The U.K. Super Team celebrated by sharing a lot of good treats with all of us. Good timing because we were super hungry. Yummy! We were all stuffed.

The China team was quite fast at learning. The India team was super smart; they knew what to do with the equipment even before we explained. The Japan team was truly well-disciplined, and the U.K. team was very brave. Wow, so much to learn from everyone around the world.

It was time for us to get back. We got back just in time since mom just tried calling me on my phone. Phew! I am home.

Our world trips continued for the next four days in a similar way, but we did have two emergency assignments in between. One was the attack by Bully Bats and the other by Sneaky Serpents. But we knew exactly what to do and, of course, Super Sushi was only getting better with every assignment. Who would have thought that this tiny cute button could be such a brave super hero? I am so proud of him.

Phew, what a tiring week!

But guess what? We now have the whole world covered. Hooray!!

Pop had a big grin. "Guys, I am so proud of you. This would have been the best day for Dr. Freckles."

We were all super proud of ourselves. We congratulated Sushi for his excellent idea. Now if there's a problem anytime - anywhere in the world - and there is no one to help, we have our Super Heroes at work!

CHAPTER

07

What Next?

I woke up quite exhausted the next morning. Sushi was just waking.

Yumm, I smell pancakes. I can't wait for breakfast. I quickly got ready and ran straight to the kitchen. And guess what? Sushi beat me there, waiting for his share. He loves sugar.

It was a beautiful day. I rode my bicycle to the Secret Base, while Sushi and Trixie tagged along.

I think Sushi and Trixie loved talking to humans, so as soon as we got to the Secret Base, they ran and put on their costumes.

"Good morning, guys!" Pop greeted. "Well, you all had a long week. I hope we don't get any new assignments today."

"I hope not," Super Sushi said.

Terrific Trixie chimed in. "Pop, you know we all feel so bad that you stay here all by yourself. We are all a team now; can't you stay with us?"

I agreed. "That's a good idea, Trixie. You know, Pop, you are small enough to disguise yourself as a toy. I have a huge toy room with a toy house just the right size for you. You can stay with us."

"Wow! That sounds very tempting! But I need to be here to take care of the Secret Base and handle all the messages from around the world."

"How about at least one day a week? I am sure you will have all your remotes to get the messages, and we all live so close by. It will be easy for you," Super Sushi said.

"Well, hmmm. Okay, that might work," Pop said thoughtfully.

Everyone cheered. "Yaaayyyy!"

It has indeed been a great start to the summer vacation. I am sure there are many more adventures to happen and Team Super Sushi can't wait.

I think all of us are super heroes from within; we just need to be brave enough to bring them out. I strongly believe that if each one of us does our little bit to help, together we can make this world a better place. I hope all of you will give it a try.

Just remember, you are never too small or weak to make a difference.

Until next time, goodbye from Super Sushi, Terrific Trixie and Kool Krithi.

Lightning Source UK Ltd.
Milton Keynes UK
UKRC02n2147011018
329839UK00016B/767